ABHIJIT MAITY

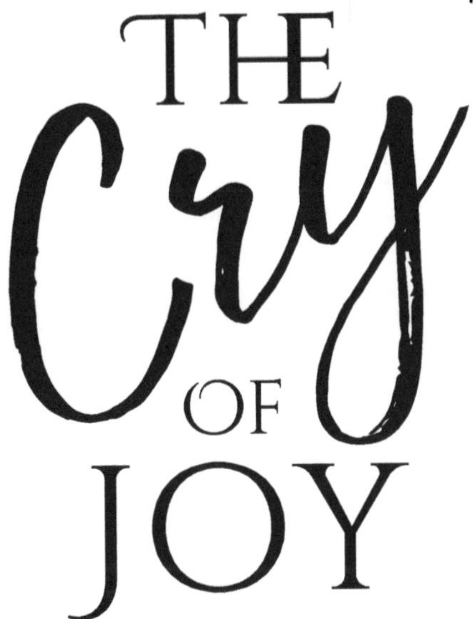

THE Cry OF JOY

A COLLECTION OF TWENTY FIVE POEMS

First Published in July 2019

ISBN: 978-93-5347-588-8

BLUEROSE PUBLISHERS (New Delhi)
www.bluerosepublishers.com
info@bluerosepublishers.com
+91 8882 898 898

Cover Design:
Mohit Joshi

Typographic Design:
Namrata Saini

Distributed by: BlueRose, Amazon, Flipkart, Shopclues

For my parents and my beloved

With thanks to
those who loved me and hurt me

Contents

Preface .... ***ix***

Prologue .... ***xi***

When There Would Be no More Breathes 1

Though I Have Many Lives to Live 2

The Thorns of Rose 3

The Fallen Leaves 5

The Leaden Eye 6

When I am Helpless 7

Who am I ? 8

I cannot Be One 10

The Convict No. 143 11

A Sigh 13

No Man's Deed 14

Relationship 15

The Class 16

When I See the Clouds 17

Pleasure in Pain 18

Unrecorded Time 19

Unending 20

To the Moon 21

The Child in Me 23

What I am Not 25

Clouds 26

He is Sick Too 27

When I Feel You 28

Other 29

The Waste Life 30

Epilogue ***31***

THE CRY OF JOY

Preface

In many poems, I have expressed my feelings of uneasiness of the age, or of some personal experiences. The unease and pain become so unacceptably familiar to our lives that we are confused about the meaning of true existence. Are we not surely confused? What is the basic purpose of our living? Are we living at all, really, or surviving? Perhaps, I am an optimist with little hopes.

These thoughts always wonder me, and I know, it has wondered many more. In these poems, I tried to give shape to my unformed thoughts, sometimes confused.

One thing I want to tell you secretly, though it is to be the job of a critic, and that, when a thought filters through my mind, it swiftly flutters through words on pages. But sometimes, when I read it later, I find in it a Keatsian tunes and Byronic intensity

A. Maity

Without you, I am:

a skeleton without flesh,
a heart without emotions,
a body without soul,
a form without contents,
a brain without thoughts,
and a life without history.

When There Would Be no More Breathes

When there would be no more breathes to take,
Silence will pour in each heart a deep distress,
And the darkness of lonely night will toll the ring
Of my unfinished tale:
Your heart would throb in mine absence.

When the eternal fingers of time's perennial race
Losing the centre of every centre and the earth's surface,
Will stop sticking forever and die childless; there—
With those soft trembling lips, you will spell my name.

When on earth I shall demise, and be lost into the air:
Every single tune of my heart's broken lyre
Will sing the unfathomed rhythm of your love,
And be a sold slave in your heart's empire.

When each word will turn against it's father,
When the vicious desire of deceivers will hit
The breast of the sky to rape each bright star,
Find me then; I shall still be there to be yours forever.

When the world will die in deathless mourn,
Each sweet soul will forget how to live on,
I, on that lifeless desert will live in strained eye
With those memories that will never ever die.

Though I Have Many Lives to Live

Though I have many lives to live,
On this barren land and to time's lone futurity,
I go on and go on, but in tireless brain I see:
From here to the rest of this unseen world,
How little I do exist and how trifle I am to be.
Though I have many tunes to sing,
Like the unending ringlets of waves in glee,
To play in full, each time I tried in vain,
In vain and in vain how many times I tried.

Nothing to sing, no life to live:
For the yelling of these ignorant words,
And the denial of life's insignificant breaths,
We never realize how meaningless is all our follies,
To stick to our unquenchable quest for happiness
And to die quietly with distorted images and painful glories.

The Thorns of Rose

I fall again into the unknown maze,
where pities do swarm,
like worms in deep darkness.

What can I do
if the waves get hurt as rains fall?

How ignorant we are:
At dawn we dream life to be
the swift water of a crystal stream,

I fight with me, in me,
to kill, to torture, to destroy
The part that hurts most,
Is it in me or in you? I know not.
I know not to kill me or to kill you,
still I know things among few
that I am a sky colourless,
a water waveless, a lyre toneless,
a body boneless, or a life breathless,
without the bitter unrest of your feelings.

I cry each time I smile,
I fall each time I stand,
I am hurt each time I love,
I die each time I revive;

Yet I waited, and still waiting:

passed million seconds and still millions to pass,
perhaps, to the fall of last human tear,
to the last drop of dried oceans,
just to embrace the presumptuous moment,
the slithering second of past and present
to catch it in the unpredictable future.

And perhaps then-
all these gentlest memories
of my love will become a child's play
on the dusty lane of your
life's asymmetrical thorny way.

The Fallen Leaves

There was a little tree:
from its birth it dreams to be
a tall to taller and someday the tallest,
through many rises and falls of lives,
to stand more than a century—
defending the stuff of storms
and rains, darkness and dim,
the fires floating by clime,
it feels the strength of struggle in vein,
to pour the world full with its breath.

But, the light is put out by a stranger
taking away the yellow dreams and soothing power,
that worms feed on its shattered heart.
only the faded leaves are fallen apart.

The Leaden Eye

The flowers of Heaven are in the sky,
How far from this uneasy world
At the unfiled pointless distance,
Running with time with their eyes.

Are they crying or scorning our cries?
If in dark clouds or in fiery winds
Like us in love-lone minds.

Many days spent, many breaths lost
Since the first till unknowable last.

How this world has itself changed!
From the unlettered, unworn, uncivilized,
Has shaped like a stone losing its rough edges,
From unformed letters like husks strewing
On water, a sentence now we have become.

But with the coming age I see
Moany minds in despair,
No hope to live, to die seems better,
Now to stare at the sky cannot feel one glee,
Is there the star that my eyes are fixed at,
Or at the blind spot in between?

When I am Helpless

If word is the life of lamish sound on earth,
It's the cause of destruction of life too:
Never did I realise the falsity of word's trace,
Like the Janus but with so many faces;

I thought love the ultimate destiny of unfitted being,
The heavenly cloth on a barely naked Spring,
O Love! O Love! How fair thy petals page,
Why thou art so queer so fairly strange?

Was I innocent like a helpless child at mother's breast
Believing myself to be the only purely dearest?
Is it an illusion my happy steps do cry to follow?
Or a rainbow whose ethereal bliss mine heart does bow?

Like a straw I'm lost delved deeply into an unknown stream
Life is nothing but an absurd incomplete dream.

Who am I?

Once I asked myself:
who am I?
Nothing came in my ignorant brain,
Silence I ruminate over
lacking proper word, proper meaning.

I asked my mother:
who am I?
She answered I'm mad,
I asked my father:
who am I?
He replied I'm a child,
I asked my elders:
who am I?
They told I am naughty,
I asked the others:
who am I?
I got nothing in reply.

Since then it started
And still it's not ended.

I ask the Sun, I ask the stars, I ask the sky:
who am I?
They suggest me to see the sea nearby.
I ask the sea:
who am I?

I can only hear
its roar and murmuring cry.

I wander into the field
and sit under a tree, tired and lonely,
in a moment the unknown *I* inside me
again starts torturing
then who am I?
decide to ask the god, finally,
and I ask the grave:
who am I?
Silence is the only reply.

I cannot Be One

I cannot be one that lewd eyes do catch,
O! What a magic thou made me not to match;
I know love beyond any corporeal trace,
Why but thee nothing imprisons my choice?

Yes, thou art unique, knows my heart,
I scorn the creator for the exquisite part.
It must have been a divine hand,
For I find Madonna, Diana, Helen in thee stand?

The rippling fragrances madden me uneasy,
All my days and nights what can I think but thee?
Something calls me, and I fly above the sky
Such roaming Romeo makes others to spy?

Let thy life be my god, and thy love my grace,
Let me feel the heaven and leave the rest in distress.

The Convict No. 143

It was a prisoner,
it was a murderer,
people knew him an insane.
Still it looked like man, felt like man,
no one believed that,
to them, it was a no man;

Yet beneath its hide,
it hides, unwillingly, unintentionally,
a small world in a candle light
And his own world known to none,

It had been sunlight years ago,
a garden of hopes with thousands colours
Until the day which threw all in strife;

In the spring of his days,
he was calm with Shree,
she was something more than life
to him, one life is too small to love
such artistic creation
and the heaven's gift,
she replaced the mother
he had lost at eight.
the girl was the reason
to live or to die.

Now everything seems
worthless since the day
he gently kissed
and cruelly killed her for betray,
thus threw his life into astray.

Now it is lifeless body and a number.

A Sigh

I am tired and my thoughts are fluttered,
I cannot see objects in beauteous forms before me;
Nature fails to mollify, to pacify turning waves of my heart,
I only loved, but am digressed, fallen apart.

The Cuckoo madly sings, but never finds the Spring,
For the breeze the flower waits its head to be tossing;
The sky waits with its wide-stretched bowed arms,
But the Night passes – the Moon forgets to come;

In river the water stands still for the ebb to begin,
Why life ever seems to be a play of fall and return?
The writer waits here for, the character is missing,
Life without your Love is not at all worth living.

If my world remains unchanged and just the same,
I'll be lost into desert, and you'll leave a sigh of my name.

No Man's Deed

Who is a poet?

A poet is He,
who can see
the invisibility,
in whose thoughts lie
limitless ocean and distanced sea,
to whom the world stands up an easel
to colour things on beyond the impossible.

He be read, discovered, his thoughts be rethought
Yet to all, he knows, he is nothing but what he is not.

Relationship

All are silly and falsely told,
Life is a liar's vow worthless in old,
To be or not to be is not really the question,
To die or to survive is the question in confusion;

We build to destroy or destroy to build,
We learn to forget or forget to learn,
We stand to fall or fall to stand again,
We lose to win or win to lose in turn;

Yet, some relationships come and leave
Like the distanced rainbow and the busy wind,
But the mark of its colours and fragrances
Remains painted forever on the wall of mind;

World is sick, full of broken promises rolling stones,
Life in it is like flowing wave whose run unknown,
We stand in smile to see it coming in ringlet
But in seconds away for a new one to be shown,

So are we—
Being habituated to waves one after another,
Try to forget unreadily the one just met and left.

The Class

When I was a schoolboy,
it never occurred to me
the masked colours of Class,
what i felt was the divisions,
from one to others in rooms or benches,
And the ones came first were yearly rewarded.

I am in a class one day.
The other day, I heard my pal in another,
who are given money
by the *Sarkars*. To these classes,
by giving the some silly sum, they say
they make the poor richer.
Is it really the matter?

That at every stage there,
they make them remember,
that you are really poorer and never be richer,
Since surviving on the mercy of the sympathizer;
if everybody is equal and fair,
why these classifications occur?
If a single vote is everyone's power,
why is it not so from the richest to a beggar?
All is to be fed equal milk of our Mother;
if rights lay by for everybody's favour,
why are they made bigger or smaller?

When I See the Clouds

When I see the clouds on a rainy day,
And breathe the odour of my fascination
To be driven out and find myself at the bay,
Towards the bending bow of the limitless sky
That touches somewhere there the breast
Of the bay. Reminds me of thousands it inspires before,
Still like the lost mussel caught between undulate water
And unnumbered creeping sands without rest,

It also reminds me of the thousands in distress.

Pains of the childless mothers
Who have sons and daughters but none to look at,
Cries of the motherless child, of the jobless youths,
Of the powerless system, of the of the sightless eyes,
Of the loveless hearts, of the odourless flowers,
Of the characterless narratives and rhythmless verse.
Perhaps the same cries that were heard once
By Sophocles at Aegean or Arnold at Dover.

I return in my mind's eye and find—
Myself caught behind the stiff bars
Of this semi-transparent window
With uneasy wind telling me of tireless hopes in mind.

Pleasure in Pain

The world can hardly imagine:
The time, here they come from Divine,
The time when universe receive one to shine
The time when Her world fills in the utmost pain,

The time when faces fade in her brain,
The time when whole family feels sustain,
The time when all the words as rain
If fall, be a little to describe the real pain,

The time, a fraction of second when
If works wrong, darkness bids the newcomer's brain,
The time when affliction reaches its crux
Every sad and remorse mixed before and become fuss,

The time the world can hardly imagine-
Even tho' after that deepest sense they spent,
Society sounds their frailty and infirmity in terms.
Shame on you that torture real creator, but follow His dictums.

Unrecorded Time

Everything in this world we know
Has a beginning and an ending of grow,
But of the birth of Time all are blind;
No documents nor any trace of thought find;
Still we know this well
Under its whirling wheel we fall.

With its razor edge fading everything by age,
All written or unwritten feelings it has power to erase.

It has the supreme power
That can smash the zenith of tower
Down to the dust never able to stare;

In life, it favours one golden chance
With that one can be hero by his entrance,
Or, sometimes it takes our favoured ones
Which leave us into the unknown lanes.

Unending

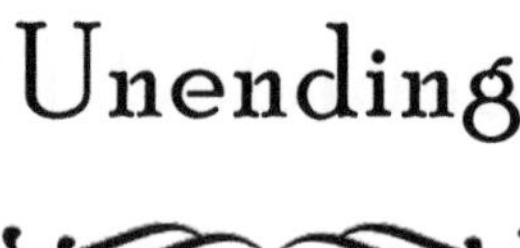

In the droplets of falling tears,
In pain passing the night airs,
How meaningful each drop is!
How sad it hides everyone's eyes.
Among those unruly stupid tears
I found myself lost—torn in fear.
I see my lifeless corpse—there,
On the dreadful desert in utter despair.

But if, every living being is a lifeless corpse,
Each soothing word is crowned with false:
Written or unwritten we know not,
In the yellow pages of crippling memories.

Still we dream, still we live, still we delude our future
With certainties in tomorrow for moment to be better.

To the Moon

O, the Moon can you hear?
Today, my cries, without any near,
O, Unlike you, the most miserable Moon
I've tasted life's beauty, the heave's nectar,
My days are gone and am left alone;
You have failed to make a love!
Thousands should die for you fair beauty,
Still your aim must prove your futility.

Though you'll have to run as have been
For many years on this bare legs akin,
Through the cloudy, dusky, rainy, shiny,
Through thunder and lightning,
Through pains and pleasure unrelenting.
Unknown, unnoticed, and unappreciated by all.
But, sure my heart I never be failure,
I have all, never to be queer, in a little compare.

I know, when I look at you, O the moon!
I am also looked at on the invisible mirror
Of you, for, another of me, somewhere there
Also with her beating heart stares at you,
O the moon, then, you will be the centre of two-halves
The source of many implacable desires,
Centring the two legs long been straddled apart.

See, the eternally lonely Self, see.
You then give us the opportunity
To love, to see, to cheer and happy to be,
O, the moon, please, enshrine me
With your blessing so I can ever her be.

The Child in Me

Once I was stammering
onto the stony night there,
I do not know how,
was truly terribly in fear,
the child in me
crying silently, cannot bear:
perhaps, my eyes are to blame
for the pillow wet in tear.

I walked away
from the stone and dark, found near
a turn—so deep an illusion,
but seemed to be darkly clear;
onto the thorny edges
of love, the gentle feet were
Unaccustomed to the danger,
that dost slave my heart and tear.

I felt starry moonlit night
better than the cloudy day,
to be hurt is an immanent undeniable thing
of love's unconquered bay;
I find my mother in you,
and the sick child at times does say:
If I fall asleep, will you caress me forever?
And never stealthily move away?

My tender whisperings wandered,
went half-lost into the dreary air,
no one heard, cared little, all ended.
sitting beside the open-window,
everything seems quietly broken and sourly just,
Mind's telescope peers to mull
over the faults done in the past.

What I am Not

Seeing this wound so deep
you console me to treat:

I said, "Are you a doctor?"
You said, "You are my guinea pig,"
I said, "Are you a scientist?
You said," I'm your doctor".
I said, "Will u cut my heart out?"
You said, "I shall heal it".

Then the time passes as water flows,
But the flow of pain is now so slow;
Still I dreamt of becoming the sunflower,
And you made me a rose with many thorns.

I called my mother to create me anew,
She said I'm already done,
And left nothing for her in due.

Day by day, in such as a special and lovely way,
Each time I fight with my inside that I am,
And the outside that you have made,
I digest the mask you put on in my stomach.

I burn myself like a candle still lighten others,
I am killing myself to make you survive,
I am hurting myself to make you feel love.

Clouds

In life when everything starts retreating,
days seems to be night with no glittering,
When I am languished
by the impaired moments in past,
and time fettered me like left pebbles on shore,
I felt my world empty and bored.

In my mind, words rush
like busy dusts before storms.
Words of those great minds,
who for so long demised but not died.
Death is not the end of all,
but the beginning of another life.

Then, they lighten my night and up I stir,
In my vacant coldness, bring a warmly fire.

He is Sick Too

A boy travelled through his lonely life,
stealing sleepy mussels from time's treasury,
his mind wandered without any strife,
sometimes to high up the sky,
sometimes to the depth of the ocean,
or to the white dusty road
leading to uncertain destiny.

But one day, touched by a magic stick,
he woke up to a painless land of delight:
something he never imagined,
something that has made him sick,
with loneliness love began to fight.

He only felt and felt but little thought:
today's smiles are the cost of tomorrow's cries,
with past hurts painted on the pages of memories,
now, still, he wanders, in wonder,
parts lost among the wrongs and rights.
But never to end life in supple certainties.

He never wanted to feel the magic
Unless the magic made him feel so,
Now, he never wants to leave the magic
nonetheless the magic left him alone so.

When I Feel You

When clouds crowded the heart's limitless sky,
Maimed the most parts of the corporeal frame,
Stabbing the soft secret walls of the soul,
Suddenly I wake up in a shelterless space: I cry.

I cried in silence, in absence, deeply,
Many a times, to defeat the pains of fragment,
Like a skull down the field I's empty, lonely.

My empty bowl filled with oceanic happiness
I saw a smiling face on the mirror of my reflection,
My sense, then, turns to the little drops of fogs
on soft crimson petals of maiden rose;
My eyes to those of the remaining uncounted stars;
My hands to the haze of misty woods at long,
I found life where everything seems quite unreal,
Still felt heaven in this shameless chaotic hell.

Other

The moanful moon is showing her
The way to live – to survive so far,
In pains, she paints the canvas without light,
Floating on the shore of surreal night,
From evil to evil very hard she bears,
Even, each moment too brutal to remember,
She has seen the false world not from afar.

The child marked her way to merry land,
Quitted to the dangers of this dreary world.

The moment her mother slapped her,
She first realized herself apart from others,
For, she looked the prettiest among the rest.
She learnt, then, how to be a woman best.
Her rosy checks were blushed in anger,
Or, in fear of all unconquered hopes in future.

The Waste Life

Let us die,
then, you and I:
the world is no place for us,
full of dreadful dreams to go by,

We all are ignorant walkers,
staggering with miscarriage life
towards the fate's uncertainty,
without love, without faith
within an unforgivable labyrinth.

You are killing me to live,
and I am loving you to die.

God has died years ago,
and He left us like a motherless child,
is it safe for you and me
to live on colourless pages
where words are not free?

Life is no life:
if death does happiness to come.
Let us sleep, then, you and I.

Epilogue

"In my beginning is my end"_ T. S. Eliot

This is not the end but the beginning-
of a new page, of a new history,
and of a new door to terrible uncertainties.

In my end is my beginning

www.ingramcontent.com/pod-product-compliance
Ingram Content Group UK Ltd.
Pitfield, Milton Keynes, MK11 3LW, UK
UKHW040013200726
13854UKWH00001B/186

9 789353 475888